EARTHQUAKE ESCAPE

J. BURCHETT & S. VOGLER

STONE ARCH BOOKS
a capstone imprint

Wild Rescue books are published by Stone Arch Books
A Capstone Imprint
1710 Roe Crest Drive,
North Mankato, Minnesota 56003
www.capstonepub.com

First published by Stripes Publishing Ltd.
1 The Coda Centre
189 Munster Road
London SW6 6AW
© Jan Burchett and Sara Vogler, 2012
Interior art © Diane Le Feyer of Cartoon Saloon, 2012

Library of Congress Cataloging-in-Publication Data
Burchett, Jan.
Earthquake escape / written by Jan Burchett [and] Sara Vogler ; illustrated by
Diane Le Feyer ; cover illustration by Sam Kennedy.
p. cm. -- (Wild rescue)
Originally published: London : Stripes, 2009.
ISBN 978-1-4048-6891-5 (library binding)
1. Twins--Juvenile fiction. 2. Brothers and sisters--Juvenile fiction. 3. Giant
panda--China--Sichuan Sheng--Juvenile fiction. 4. Wildlife conservation--China--
Sichuan Sheng--Juvenile fiction. 5. Wenchuan Earthquake, China, 2008--Juvenile
fiction. 6. Sichuan Sheng (China)--Juvenile fiction. 7. Adventure stories. [1.
Twins--Fiction. 2. Brothers and sisters--Fiction. 3. Giant panda--Fiction. 4. Pandas-
-Fiction. 5. Wildlife conservation--Fiction. 6. Wenchuan Earthquake, China,
2008--Fiction. 7. Sichuan Sheng (China)--Fiction. 8. China--Fiction. 9. Adventure
and adventurers--Fiction.] I. Vogler, Sara. II. Le Feyer, Diane, ill. III. Kennedy,
Sam, 1971- ill. IV. Title.
PZ7.B915966Ear 2012
823.914--dc23   2011025559

Cover Art: Sam Kennedy
Graphic Designer: Russell Griesmer
Production Specialist: Michelle Biedscheid

Design Credits: Shutterstock 51686107 (p. 4-5),
Shutterstock 51614464 (p. 148-149, 150, 152)

Printed in the United States of America in Stevens Point, Wisconsin.
042013
007301R

TABLE OF CONTENTS

WILD RESCUE

MISSION

BEN WOODWARD
WILD Operative

ZOE WOODWARD
WILD Operative

TARGET: ◎

BRIEFING

CODE NAME: JING-JING

CHAPTER 1

LIFT-OFF!

Ben's mountain bike soared through the air. "Woohoo!" he yelled. As he landed, he glanced back at his twin sister, Zoe. She was catching up to him. Their mountain bikes — gifts from their grandma — were brand-new. A race across this hillside was a perfect way to try them out.

Pedaling faster, Ben swerved around a tree root. As he turned, he skidded across a patch of mud, barely avoiding a crash.

As Ben breathed a sigh of relief, Zoe took the opportunity to catch up. Her pedals circled in a blur as she sprinted down the steep slope. The shallow stream at the bottom was their finish line. Grandma was sitting in her car near the ravine, reading a book while waiting for them to return.

Grandma lived with Ben and Zoe during summer vacations while their parents were away. Their parents were vets whose jobs had them traveling all around the world. Ben and Zoe usually went with them, but this trip would keep their parents away until after school had started. So the twins had to stay home this time.

Zoe splashed through the stream, cheering triumphantly. "I win!" she cried.

Ben was splattered in mud. He grinned as he zoomed up behind Zoe.

"You got lucky," Ben said. "Just wait until next time!"

Suddenly, a whirring sound echoed through the area. The nearby trees began to sway from side to side. The teens stopped talking and looked upward. Directly overhead, they saw the whirring rotor of a helicopter. The next instant, two harnesses on ropes dropped down just in front of them.

"What's going on?" asked Ben.

Zoe's face lit up. "I recognize that helicopter," she yelled. "It's Uncle Stephen!"

Ben and Zoe's uncle, Dr. Stephen Fisher, ran a top secret organization called WILD. It was dedicated to rescuing endangered animals all over the world — and Ben and Zoe were its youngest, and newest, operatives.

Ben grabbed one of the harnesses. "We'd better get up there and see what mission Uncle Stephen has for us this time!" he said.

The twins strapped themselves in. Soon they were being lifted into the air, high above the trees and hills.

Zoe gasped. "What about our bikes?" she yelled over the deafening sound of the rotor blades.

Ben looked down at a small figure on the ground. Their grandmother was waving up at them as they made their dizzying ascent.

"Grandma has it under control," Ben yelled, waving back at her. "After all, she knows what Uncle Stephen has in store for us before we do!"

CHAPTER 2

GEARED UP

Inside the helicopter, Ben and Zoe strapped on their seatbelts and pulled on their headsets. The pilot's familiar face peered back at the twins. "Good morning," she said. "As you can see, your uncle has another job for you."

Zoe sniffed the air, smelling a familiar scent. Their uncle had designed the helicopter to run on chicken manure. It was environmentally friendly, but it smelled awful.

"Nice to see you again, Erika!" said Zoe, plugging her nose. "Where's Uncle Stephen sending us this time?"

"I can't tell you that," Erika said. She smiled and passed Zoe an envelope. Although Erika was their uncle's second-in-command, and she had all the information he did, she knew their eccentric uncle would want to explain their mission to them personally.

Ben snatched the envelope from Zoe and plunged his hand inside. "I bet I know what's inside," he said. "Another glass eye!"

Zoe nodded. "A message explaining the next rescue mission, you mean," she agreed.

Sure enough, a glass eye fell from the envelope into Ben's hand.

"What kind of animal has an eye like this?" Ben asked. "It has a slit pupil."

"There's one simple way to find out," Erika said, pointing. "It fits inside that console over there."

Ben placed the eye into a small hollow space in the helicopter's dashboard. At once, a hologram of a man wearing a Hawaiian shirt appeared. "Greetings, my nephew and niece!" he said. "You know the drill by now, so I'll be brief. I'm sending you two to China. A giant panda cub is in trouble and needs our assistance. I'll have more details for you upon your arrival." Their uncle grinned wide, and then the hologram blipped out.

"A giant panda," cried Zoe. "They're the cutest things ever!"

"Not so cute if it sat on you," joked Ben. "A fully grown one weighs more than two hundred pounds. They have to eat for about fifteen hours a day just to stay alive."

"Sounds like you!" Zoe said, laughing.

"Pretty much," Ben agreed. "And they're seriously endangered. Their main diet is bamboo, but lots of bamboo forests have been cut down."

Zoe rolled her eyes. "I already knew that," she said. "I know everything about pandas. They're my favorite animals."

Ben smirked. "Well, you didn't know they have slit pupils," he said.

"Whatever!" said Zoe.

The helicopter headed north across the choppy sea toward Uncle Stephen's remote island.

As soon as they'd landed and climbed out, Erika clicked a button on the ground. A fake shed rose up to conceal the helicopter from outside eyes.

Without waiting for Erika, Zoe and Ben ran over to an outhouse. Zoe flung open the ratty door and they all crammed in. The bathroom became a secret elevator. "Hold on to your stomach!" Ben joked as they sped deep underground.

The door to the elevator shaft swung open, and Ben and Zoe hurried along the brightly lit hallway. They placed their fingertips on an ID pad next to a door marked CONTROL ROOM.

"Print identification confirmed," came an electronic voice. The door slid open and Ben and Zoe dashed into the huge room. High-tech plasma screens covered the walls.

Uncle Stephen swung around in his chair. "That was quick!" he said. "Glad to see you're as fast as ever."

Zoe ran to her uncle and gave him a hug. "Tell us about the panda," Zoe said eagerly. "How can we help?"

Uncle Stephen led the twins to the largest monitor. He touched it, bringing up an image of a solemn panda cub sitting on a tree stump. "This is Jing-Jing."

"He's adorable!" gushed Zoe.

Ben rolled his eyes. "There she goes again," he said, groaning. Ben loved animals just as much as his sister, but there were times when she just got too mushy.

The image changed to a satellite map of China. Then it zoomed in on a thickly wooded mountainous area.

It began focusing on a group of buildings and fenced areas. The mountains rose up steeply on both sides.

Erika joined the briefing. "Jing-Jing lives at the Ningshang Sanctuary," she said. "It's in the Sichuan Province of western China."

"Wasn't there an earthquake there last month?" asked Zoe.

"Indeed there was, Zoe," their uncle said. "And the sanctuary was badly damaged."

"Luckily, all the pandas were saved," their uncle continued, "but there's a lot of rebuilding that still needs to be done."

Erika touched the screen toolbar. The image changed to a video clip of several young pandas slowly climbing a metal frame.

"We don't have any footage of Jing-Jing," Erika told them, "but here are some other one-year-old panda cubs in the panda cub compound. They're orphans and have lived there most of their lives. Pandas aren't really independent until they're two years old and able to find food for themselves. Only then are they released into the wild."

Zoe watched the cubs tumble awkwardly down a slide.

"They're like clumsy little teddy bears!" Zoe said.

"Since the earthquake in the Sichuan Province, WILD has been worried about the safety of the animals there," Erika said. "We thought the sanctuary pandas would be fine, but five days ago we discovered that Jing-Jing had escaped through a break in the compound's damaged fencing."

"Did the sanctuary send out a search party?" Zoe asked.

"Certainly," said Uncle Stephen. "But they found no signs of him and had to give up. They don't have enough workers there to spare for such a task."

Ben nodded. "I guess they must be busy repairing things and trying to keep all the other pandas safe," he said.

"You're right," said Erika. "And aftershocks are causing more problems. Everyone out there is struggling to get things back to normal."

Zoe frowned. "If Jing-Jing's too young to forage, then he won't survive on his own," she said.

Uncle Stephen nodded. "And he'll be very scared," he added.

"Then we'd better get to China as soon as we can," said Ben. "Let's get packed!"

Uncle Stephen beamed. "I knew I could rely on you two," he said.

He rifled through a messy drawer in his desk and pulled out what looked like two handheld game consoles. He handed them to Ben and Zoe. "But you can't leave without your BUGs!"

The BUGs were incredibly useful.

They could be used to communicate with WILD HQ, track animals, translate languages, and do tons of other things that Ben and Zoe still hadn't figured out how to use.

Uncle Stephen handed them a couple of slim flashlights. "And you might want these," he said. "These are FINs — Fisher Integrated Nanofirers. They'll be useful in the mountains."

"A new invention?" asked Ben. "Show me what it does!"

"Not in here!" Erika said quickly. "It's designed to be used outside."

"You're no fun, Erika!" Uncle Stephen teased. "Anyway, there's more. I've been busy inventing a few other new things." He handed them a pair of complicated-looking goggles.

"These are thermogoggles," he said. "They will allow you to track animals by heat."

Their uncle then handed them a pair of lightweight backpacks. "And these should come in handy for carrying all your new gear."

Ben and Zoe fidgeted with the new toys excitedly. "Cool!" they said in unison.

"Remember," Uncle Stephen warned, "terrain in those mountains is dangerous even under the best of conditions. There may still be aftershocks as they can occur up to a year after a quake. Make sure you keep yourselves safe."

Erika chimed in. "I'll brief you on earthquakes on the way there," she said. "In the meantime, get packed — we're heading out immediately!"

CHAPTER 3

MR. ZHI

Ben and Zoe arrived in China at a private airstrip outside Chengdu. From there, Erika drove them over cracked and potholed Sichuan roads to the little village in a deep valley next to a fast-flowing river. It was very late when they arrived at the Panda Palace Hotel — a simple guest house that had been damaged by the earthquake. Part of its roof was missing, and only one bathroom was working right.

The owner, Yao Zhi, gave them a warm welcome, despite looking surprised to have guests so soon after the earthquake.

After he woke up the next morning, Ben pushed open the bedroom window and gazed up at the densely wooded mountains, which stretched as far as his eye could see. "I can't wait to start our search for Jing-Jing," he said, eagerly pulling on his boots. "Let's go!"

Zoe strapped on her new backpack. "Jing-Jing could be anywhere," she said. "If you charge off without a plan, you'll get lost. We have to go to the sanctuary first and get some intel."

Ben stuffed his BUG into his pocket. "But what if we don't get any useful intel there?" he said. "We'll have wasted precious time."

"The workers there know Jing-Jing well," said Zoe. "We should be able to find some useful information, like his favorite food, weight and height — that sort of thing."

Ben opened the door and waited for Zoe to follow. "Fine," he said. "But remember, we're just kids on vacation with their parents. They can't know why we're really here."

"Well, duh," Zoe said. She grabbed their waterproof jackets from the table. "We're going to need these. Erika said it can rain at any time here."

"We should warn the hotel owner that we might not be back tonight," Ben suggested. "Otherwise he might think we got lost or something and report us missing."

"Good thinking!" said Zoe.

As they reached the front desk downstairs, Ben handed the room key to Mr. Zhi. "I hope you enjoyed your breakfast," the man said.

Ben grinned. "It was delicious!" he said. They had eaten steamed buns filled with lamb.

Mr. Zhi smiled. "Your aunt left earlier today," he said. "You were still asleep, I think."

"Aunt Erika has to do some work in Chengdu," Zoe explained quickly. "We're used to traveling on our own."

Erika had actually gone off to another devastated area to check on the wildlife there. The hotel owner looked a little worried, but he said nothing.

Ben and Zoe had to be careful that no one suspected why they were really there. Everyone had to believe that they were on vacation with their eccentric aunt.

"We're going to visit the Ningshang Panda Sanctuary," Zoe told him. "I've always wanted to see the giant pandas."

Mr. Zhi smiled in relief. "That's a great idea!" he said. "You'll be safe there without your aunt."

"She's meeting us there later," said Ben. "She wants to take us on an overnight trip. We'll be away for the night, but probably back tomorrow."

Mr. Zhi nodded. "Where are you going?" he asked.

"We don't know," Zoe said quickly. "It's a surprise."

Mr. Zhi smiled. "Wait one moment," he said. "I'll give you a packed lunch."

He reached underneath the counter and produced two bulging paper bags. "Stuffed pancakes," the man said, smiling.

Ben's eyes lit up. "Thanks!" he said, happily slipping them into his backpack.

CHAPTER 4

XU MEI

Zoe and Ben followed the river out of the village toward the sanctuary. They walked over dry, cracked ground. Half-collapsed buildings lined both sides of the road. There were many workers clearing and demolishing the rubble, calling out to each other in Chinese.

Zoe struggled to pull out the squidgy little earpiece from her BUG. "We'd better put in our translators," she said.

"What dialect did Erika say they speak around here?" Ben asked.

"Sichuanese," Zoe said. She pressed her earpiece into her ear and listened to the workers speak. "That's interesting," she said with a grin. "They're saying, 'Who's that ugly boy on the other side of the road?'"

Ben frowned. He quickly shoved his earpiece in, listening intently to their conversations. "No, they're not!" he said. "They're complaining about the local soccer scores."

"You must've missed it, then," Zoe said, chuckling. Ben punched her playfully in the shoulder.

Soon, they came to the remains of a ruined bus shelter that had fallen into a deep hole.

Ben shook his head sadly. "It must have been really frightening for the locals when the earthquake hit," he said.

Zoe shuddered. "And utterly terrifying for the pandas," she added. "They wouldn't have understood what was going on at all."

They continued walking. The winding road led away from the houses. Soon, the high wooden fence of the sanctuary became visible. The densely forested mountains could be seen behind it. Clouds loomed around the peaks in a thick mist.

"Look over there," said Ben, pointing. "That land used to be forest, but now it has all been cleared."

"Something's being built," said Zoe. "Those poor pandas, losing their home like that. It's terrible when people don't consider the animals' needs."

Ben brought up a satellite map of the area on his BUG. He zoomed in on the Ningshang Sanctuary. "It's bigger than I thought," he said, showing Zoe. "I bet that's where Jing-Jing is."

"That doesn't help us much," said Zoe, looking at the map on the screen. "Jing-Jing could be anywhere in there. Erika said he'd been missing for five or six days now."

Moments later, they arrived at the gates of the sanctuary. It appeared to be open, but no one was at the ticket booth. They could hear workers speaking Chinese and the sounds of hammering and sawing.

Zoe peered around worriedly. "I don't see any tourists," she said. "Is it even open?"

A man in a white coat was approaching. "Can I help you?" he asked in English. There was a solemn young girl with him. She stared out from under shiny, dark bangs. She wore a blue sweatshirt with a small panda logo on it.

"We'd like to see the sanctuary, please," said Zoe.

The man gave an apologetic shrug. "I'm sorry, but our guides are all busy doing repair work," he said. "I don't like to turn visitors away, but I'm afraid there won't be any tours today."

The young girl pulled at her father's sleeve. "I can show them around, Daddy," she said. She spoke in Chinese, so Zoe and Ben had to pretend they hadn't understood what she said. "I'll keep them safe, I promise!"

"I don't think it's a good idea," said the man. "It's total chaos inside."

Ben and Zoe had no choice but to turn and walk away, hoping that the man would agree with his daughter before they had gone too far. "Walk slowly," muttered Ben.

"Please, Father?" they heard the little girl beg.

The man sighed. "Wait a minute, please!" he called out in English. Ben and Zoe spun around. "My daughter, Xu Mei, knows a lot about what we do here. She will show you around. No charge, of course."

Ben and Zoe ran back eagerly. "Thank you so much!" Zoe said. Ben smiled.

"It's settled, then," said the man.

The man patted his daughter on the head and walked off toward one of the buildings.

Xu Mei turned toward Ben and Zoe, smiling broadly. "Come with me, please!" she announced in English.

"You speak our language very well," said Zoe.

"I learn it at school," said Xu Mei. "What are your names?"

Ben smiled. "She's Zoe, and I'm Ben," he said.

Xu Mei gave them a polite nod, and then led them between two gray stone buildings into a courtyard. People in blue sanctuary sweatshirts were carrying buckets of vegetables and planks of wood around. They smiled at the children as they continued working.

Xu Mei swept her arm, trying her best to sound like a practiced tour guide. "This is the visitors' area," she announced in a practiced voice. "Here's the café and the gift shop." She pointed to her left, puffing out her chest. "And there is the information office!"

Zoe whispered to Ben, "She's adorable." Ben nodded.

A red banner with some gold Chinese characters hung over the open door where Xu Mei was pointing.

LEARN ALL ABOUT PANDAS! it read in English. Through the doorway, they could see a large, brightly lit room. Inside, display boards showed photographs and descriptions of panda life at the sanctuary.

Xu Mei nodded toward the fence. "Over there is the enclosure for the panda cubs," she said excitedly. "It's my favorite place in the whole Sanctuary. Come with me and I'll show you why!"

Zoe raced across the courtyard and looked over the fence.

The grassy compound beyond the fence was much lower than the courtyard. There were wooden huts around the edge with small entry doors. What looked like a child's climbing frame was in the center. A group of young pandas was on it, wrestling with each other. Others were lumbering about on the grass, or lazing on their backs and chewing bamboo.

"I wish I could go in and hug them all!" whispered Zoe.

"You could be their mom," teased Ben.

Xu Mei's expression grew serious. "They do need a mother," she said. "They are all orphans. These pandas are very friendly. I even go in and play with them sometimes — when a grown-up is there."

"You're so lucky," Zoe said. Xu Mei nodded, smiling.

Ben pointed at a little thicket of tall, waving plants in the corner. "That's bamboo, isn't it?" he asked. "I've read it's their favorite food. Do you give them vitamins, rice, honey, carrots, and apples, too?"

"Yes," Xu Mei said. "We give them bottles of milk, just like babies drink. These pandas will grow much bigger than pandas in the wild. Wild pandas have to eat bamboo all day just to get enough nutrition."

"Did all your pandas survive the earthquake?" asked Zoe. Ben opened his mouth to speak, but Zoe silenced him with a wink. They couldn't admit that they already knew about the lost panda. They had to hear it from Xu Mei. Keeping WILD a secret made things difficult sometimes.

"Yes," their guide said, "but they were very scared and some of the buildings fell down." Xu's face grew sad. "Then last week one of the panda cubs escaped from here. The fence was broken by an aftershock, you see."

"Oh, no" said Ben gently. "Has he been found yet?"

Xu Mei shook her head sadly. "We all searched for him, but we have no more time now. He was my favorite." Her eyes began to fill with tears. "There are clouded leopards in the forest. My father has seen one attack a wild panda before. Jing-Jing is in danger out there."

"That's terrible," said Zoe. "Do you know where he went?"

Xu Mei began to cry. Zoe felt awful. They needed to find out all they could about Jing-Jing, but she had never meant to upset her.

Zoe put her arm around Xu Mei. "Would you show us the rest of the sanctuary?" Zoe asked. "You're a very good guide."

Xu Mei smiled and wiped her eyes. "I am?" she asked excitedly.

"You are," Zoe repeated. She took Xu Mei's hand and led her toward the information office. "Let's look in here now."

Ben followed closely behind Zoe. "What are you doing?" he whispered. "If we're going to find out about Jing-Jing —"

"Shh," Zoe whispered back. "Just play along."

Ben shrugged. Zoe quickly scanned the photos on display for a picture of Jing-Jing. There were tiny pink pandas in incubators, mothers with their cubs, and a whole board of photos of young panda cubs sleeping, eating, and playing.

Unfortunately for Zoe, the pandas' names weren't listed. Then Zoe's gaze stopped at a picture on a wall-mounted board. It was the photo of a young girl cuddling a tiny baby panda while feeding it from a bottle. It was so young that its markings were only just beginning to show through its fuzzy fur.

"That's you, isn't it?" Zoe asked Xu Mei. The girl nodded. "And the panda?" Zoe added.

"Jing-Jing," Xu Mei said, almost in a whisper. "He is the one who is lost."

Xu Mei pointed to the next photo. It showed a line of tubby panda cubs with their noses digging into their feeding bowls. "Jing-Jing is the one at the end," she explained. "He was trying to steal his brother's dinner."

Xu Mei walked a few steps, then pointed at another photo. "And this one is me with Jing-Jing," she said, smiling sadly. "He is much bigger now, though. He was only a few days old when my father found him in the wild, but now he is almost two years old. His mother died when he was young."

"Jing-Jing's paw was squished when he was a baby — the paw on the left," Xu Mei explained. "It's a funny shape now, and two of his claws are missing."

Ben gave Zoe a secret thumbs up. "That might be useful," he said. Zoe nodded.

Ben moved along the display, looking at the pictures.

Zoe's way of getting the information they needed seemed to be working. "What had happened to Jing-Jing's mother?" Ben asked.

"She didn't get enough food," said Xu Mei. "The bamboo where she was living in the wild had died."

"Good thing your father found Jing-Jing when he did," said Zoe.

"Yes," said Xu Mei. "He cannot live for long on his own in the wild."

Xu's shoulders sank. "He will not know how to get food or where is safe," she said. "I wanted to go and search for him, but my father said it was too dangerous for me in the mountains."

A tear ran down Xu Mei's cheek. "Poor little Jing-Jing," she said. "I just hope his luck has not run out."

Zoe took her hand. "What if we looked for him?" she said. "Me and Ben, I mean."

Xu Mei's eyes filled with hope. "You can do that?" she said. "But how? You do not know these mountains."

"Jing-Jing may not have wandered very far," Ben said. "He could be hiding somewhere close, too scared to move."

Xu Mei's face broke into a smile. "Then I will come with you!" she said excitedly. "I will get some of Jing-Jing's food, and a feeding bottle."

Xu Mei darted out of the door before Zoe or Ben could even respond.

Zoe gently stroked the photo of the tiny panda cub, his little pink mouth guzzling at the bottle Xu Mei held for him.

"I hope we can find him," Zoe said. "It's not going to be easy."

"We'll find him," Ben said firmly. "We have to."

CHAPTER 5

ON THE HUNT

After returning with some panda food and a bottle, Xu Mei led them out of the sanctuary and straight to Jing-Jing's escape route.

Ben bent down at the side of the road to examine the boarded-up area of fencing. "So this is where Jing-Jing got out," he said.

Zoe examined the break in the fence. "He must have squeezed through," she agreed. "Did he leave any pawprints?"

Xu Mei shrugged. "Lots of people were around," she said. "We couldn't find any."

Zoe looked at the land beyond the sanctuary fence. Just on the other side of the road was a cluster of low buildings and people working in the fields among a sea of waving yellow stalks. In the distance, she could see water reflecting light in the rice fields.

"I recognize that crop," said Zoe. "It's almost full-grown. Would Jing-Jing eat that?"

Xu Mei shook her head. "He wouldn't like it," she said. "He would have kept on going."

"But what if he didn't?" said Ben. "What if he got scared and hid in a barn there, or something?"

"I doubt it," said Zoe. "The sanctuary told everyone to look for Jing-Jing. The farmer must have searched for him already."

"Yes," Xu Mei said. "But many farmers have been too busy to help since the earthquake."

"So it's possible that Jing-Jing is hiding on the farm?" asked Ben.

Xu Mei nodded eagerly.

"Let's ask the farmer if we can search," suggested Zoe.

"Mr. Chen is kind of grumpy," said Xu Mei, "and he does not speak English."

Ben grinned. "Then we're lucky that you're here!" he said. Xu Mei smiled and nodded.

The three of them walked along a wide track past a damaged barn. Zoe peered in, hoping to catch sight of the little panda, but all she saw was a pile of empty sacks and some straw. They moved on.

When they reached the farmhouse, they waited beneath the corrugated metal sheet that was hung over Mr. Chen's front door. They could hear the sounds of noisy chickens on the other side. The messy yard was full of ladders, piles of wood, and broken bricks. The ground all around was cracked and pitted from the earthquake.

"Still got your translation earpiece in?" Zoe whispered to her brother.

"You bet," Ben said.

"Remember," Zoe warned, "they can't know that we understand Chinese."

The door suddenly swung open. Xu Mei leaped back in surprise. There stood Mr. Chen, and he didn't look happy about being disturbed.

He spoke rapidly in Chinese to Xu Mei. "I know you! You come from that sanctuary. What do you want?" The translated voice was crystal clear through Zoe and Ben's BUG earpieces.

"I am so sorry to trouble you, sir," Xu Mei said politely, "and I hope you will forgive me." She stared at the ground as she spoke.

Zoe was glad that they weren't doing the negotiating. They knew so little about Chinese manners.

"We are trying to find the panda that got lost," Xu Mei said politely.

The man said nothing. "We would be so happy if you would let us look in your barn," Xu repeated politely.

Mr. Chen snorted. "Don't waste your time," he said. "I looked, and he isn't there."

All of a sudden, there was a faint rumbling sound. The ground beneath them vibrated for a few seconds. Everyone bent their knees and held out their arms to keep their balance.

Ben looked at Zoe. "Aftershock!" she said.

Dust showered down from the farmhouse roof. A piece of metal sheeting slipped down and crashed into the ground a few feet away.

Mr Chen waved them off impatiently. "Even more work for me now," he bellowed. "Leave now."

Xu Mei bowed her head politely and turned to walk away. Ben and Zoe followed.

"He says the panda isn't there," Xu Mei said. "But that we can look."

They hurried over to the barn. Inside, broken boxes and rusty tools rested on the floor. At the back, haybales were stacked high against the wall. Ben began to poke around some broken machinery in a corner while Xu Mei climbed up the mountain of haybales.

"Nothing up here," she called down.

Zoe and Ben looked through the machinery. "Look!" Zoe said suddenly. "I see white fur behind this machine."

There was a movement within the dark shadows. Xu Mei immediately leaped down to join them. She dropped to her hands and knees and wriggled under the dirty machinery. "Jing-Jing!" she called softly.

Hiss! A scrawny white cat darted past her and disappeared behind the straw.

"It was just a cat," said Zoe. "I don't think Jing-Jing is here, Xu Mei. We'd better look somewhere —"

Zoe stopped. Something had come into the barn behind them. They heard a terrifying sound that made the hairs on the back of their necks stand up on end.

CHAPTER 6

CUT LOOSE

A deep, threatening growl filled the barn. They turned slowly to see a guard dog in the doorway, its teeth bared.

It looked very strong — and angry.

"Back away, everybody," Ben muttered out of the side of his mouth. "Don't make any sudden movements."

"And don't look it in the eye," added Zoe.

Keeping their gazes lowered, the three of them shuffled backward.

The dog advanced, snarling. Its heavy chain dragged behind it.

"Good thing it's tied up," said Ben. "I don't think it can reach us."

"Yes, it can," whispered Xu Mei. "Look." At the end of the chain, a stake was being dragged across the ground.

"It must have come loose during the aftershock," Zoe said. "Climb as fast as you can!"

They scrambled up the straw mountain. The dog lunged, snapping at the air beneath their feet. Zoe felt dog slobber slap against her ankle. The dog hurled itself at the straw bales again and again, but they were too high to reach.

"We're trapped up here now!" cried Xu Mei.

Zoe looked down at the dog as it clawed away at the straw, its veins standing out from its neck. It wasn't going to give up until it had them.

"I feel a breeze on my back," Zoe said suddenly, turning to investigate. "Look, the wall's broken here!" She hooked her fingers into the split wood and pulled. It came away with a loud CRACK. The guard dog barked fiercely at the sound.

"Nice work, Zoe," said Ben. He cautiously poked his head through the opening. "We can squeeze through. There's a big drop down to the ground, but we'll have to risk it."

He edged in between the shattered planks and jumped, disappearing from sight.

Zoe looked down. Ben had landed on a pile of small logs stacked for use as kindling. He beckoned silently. Zoe and Xu Mei jumped.

The dog was nowhere to be seen, but they dashed for the fence, not daring to stop until they were off the farmer's land near the river. After checking to make sure they hadn't been followed, they sat down to get their breath back.

"No sign of Jing-Jing," said Xu Mei.

"We've only looked in one place," said Zoe. "Let's have some lunch and think about what we're going to do next." She pulled out the lunch bags Mr. Zhi had given them and offered one to Xu Mei. "Here, we got these from the guest house we're staying in."

Ben devoured his pancake filled with vegetables and chunks of chicken. "Delicious!" he said. Then he gasped. "And spicy!" He grabbed his bottle and took huge gulps of water. Xu Mei laughed.

"You must be staying at the Panda Palace Hotel," Xu Mei said through a full mouth. "My friend Wen lives there. He got hurt when the roof fell in during the earthquake."

"Is he all right?" asked Ben.

"He is in stable condition at the Chengdu Hospital," Xu Mei said. "My mother said it is a pity the new medical center is not built yet." She pointed at the stretch of deforestation Ben and Zoe had seen earlier.

"If my brother had been treated at the new facility," Xu said, "then he would have gotten help much quicker."

"We should have realized the people here have a good reason for tearing up the forest," Ben muttered to Zoe. "We were only thinking about how bad it was for the pandas."

"True," Zoe whispered back. "Chengdu is a long way to go if you're injured."

They munched away at their lunch in silence.

Xu Mei chirped up after a few minutes. "Where shall we look now?" she asked, her fingers wrapped around a bean shoot pancake. "My father said I must not go into the mountains, but I think we have to."

Zoe suddenly felt guilty. They'd already put the little girl into a dangerous situation.

Zoe would never have forgiven herself if the farmer's dog had hurt Xu Mei. They would have to continue hunting on their own.

Zoe pretended to look at her watch. "I don't think we have time for any more searching today," she said. "Aunt Erika will be expecting us."

Ben gave her a puzzled look. "But she's —"

"Waiting for us, yes," Zoe said firmly. "We have to go back to the hotel."

"But I might know where Jing-Jing could be," Xu Mei said eagerly. "Maybe he went back to where my father found him — where Jing-Jing was born." She held her hand over her eyes and looked at the mountain slope beyond the deforested land.

"It was near a big waterfall somewhere up there," Xu Mei said.

"I'm sorry, Xu Mei, but after that dog attack, I think we'd better send you home," said Zoe. She ignored Ben's shocked look.

Xu Mei's eyes filled with tears. "But you said you would find him with me!" she said.

"Maybe tomorrow," said Zoe.

"Tomorrow will be too late!" Xu Mei said, jumping up. "I thought you were my friends!"

Before Ben and Zoe could stop her, she ran away sobbing.

CHAPTER 7

ON TRACK

"Why'd you do that, Zoe?" Ben asked. "WILD sent us here to search for Jing-Jing!"

"And that's what we're going to do," said Zoe. "I know it seemed mean, but it's not safe to take a little girl with us. She could've gotten hurt by that guard dog."

Ben frowned. "I guess you're right," he said. "So what's our next step?"

"Xu Mei might be right about Jing-Jing going back to his birthplace," Zoe said.

"His birthplace is probably the best place to start looking," Ben agreed.

Ben pulled out his BUG and brought up an image of the area. He typed in "waterfall" and selected the displayed map with his finger. "This has to be it," he said. "It's the only waterfall nearby."

"But it's uphill," Zoe pointed out, "so it's going to take a lot longer than you think. We'd better get going." They stuffed the remains of their lunches into their backpacks and marched off in the direction of the forest.

Then Ben stopped suddenly. "I just realized something," he said.

"Please don't tell me you're already hungry again," teased Zoe.

"Real funny," Ben said.

"But no," Ben continued. "it's what Xu Mei said earlier — that the bamboo had all died where Jing-Jing was found," he said. "I've read about bamboo. It takes years to grow back. If Jing-Jing is in the forest, he'll have nothing to eat."

"You're right," said Zoe. "The poor thing will be starving if he's there."

Just then, Zoe noticed something under a huge tree. "Look!" she said. She ran over to the tree and crouched upon a carpet of long pine cones scattered over the ground. Several little pawprints were visible beneath the cones.

Ben ran over to join Zoe. "Panda tracks!" he said.

"Good thing, too," Zoe said wearily. "I was beginning to think we were in the wrong place."

The hour-long climb through the dense forest was exhausting. It was raining so hard that Ben and Zoe were forced to take shelter for a while. Once the rain let up, the light was fading and they still hadn't reached the waterfall.

Soon after resuming their trek, Zoe came across some more pawprints. "They're definitely panda," she said. She held the pawprint image on her display to compare it to the imprint in the soft earth. "See? Five toes, claw marks, and a pear-shaped pad — the same as on the BUG."

"Hang on," said Ben. "It's hard to see in this light." He dug through his backpack and pulled out their night goggles. He put his on. Everything was bathed in a green glow, and was much easier to see.

Ben bent down to inspect the ground. "Nice work, Zoe," he said. "These are definitely panda pawprints." Ben gently felt the marks in the earth. "And they're still fresh. They've still got sharp edges, so they must have been made recently. Jing-Jing can't be far away."

Zoe scanned the ground. "Here's another one," she said eagerly. "And another! The trail goes uphill, toward the waterfall."

"Is there a deformed print," Ben asked, "like Jing-Jing's?"

"I haven't found one yet," said Zoe, still searching. "But let's follow them. It's the only lead we have."

As they walked on through a grove of overhanging trees, a strange cry filled the air. "What's that?" whispered Zoe. "It's really creepy."

Ben held his BUG up in the air. It beeped when it determined the source of the cry.

"A clouded leopard," Ben said. "Xu Mei warned us about them. We have to be careful. They attack anything up to the size of a deer. So we'd make a perfect meal."

"Quick!" said Zoe. "Turn the scent dispersers on! Then it can't detect our smell."

Ben and Zoe pressed the keys on their BUGs. A quiet hiss spat out from the BUGs. They walked on, trying to avoid stepping on leaves and small twigs.

Ben craned his neck. "Listen," he said. "I hear the sound of water in the distance. We must be near the falls."

Zoe didn't answer. She was standing in front of a clump of tall brown stalks that stuck out from the ground at odd angles.

Dead leaves and flowers hung limply from the tall brown stalks. "What happened here?" Zoe asked.

"It's dead bamboo," Ben told her. He crumbled one of the dried, shriveled flowers in his hand. It scattered over his boots. "This is really bad news for the wild pandas."

"Do you think we've reached the area where Jing-Jing was born?" said Zoe. "Xu Mei said there was dead bamboo all around and that it was near the waterfall."

"I'm not sure," said Ben. "Let's keep following the trail."

The light gradually faded, giving way to complete darkness. Ben and Zoe pushed through the thicket of sharp stalks, their boots crunching on dead wood.

Even with their goggles on, the trail of pawprints was getting harder to follow. Zoe kept her eyes to the ground. Ben followed close behind. They could hear the distant waterfall.

"Wait, Zoe!" called Ben. "Look at this."

They squatted down beside a faint print in the mud. "It's a back paw," said Zoe. "And there are only three toes! It has to be Jing-Jing's. Maybe there are more around here somewhere."

They poked around in the bamboo, scratching their arms on the broken twigs. Suddenly there was a loud pattering above their heads. A heavy rain pounded down through the leaves. They quickly pulled on their waterproof jackets.

"The trail's disappearing," Zoe shouted. "The rain's washing away the tracks!"

"We'll go in the direction they were heading," Ben shouted back.

They hadn't gone far when the rain stopped. Now they could clearly hear the waterfall. Zoe bent over and picked up something from the ground.

"Look at this," she said, passing Ben a withered bamboo branch. "It has teeth marks in it. I bet that was Jing-Jing's."

Ben nodded. "We've got to find him," he said.

Zoe pushed through the dense bamboo stalks and stood open-mouthed at the sight in front of her. A long stream of white water was thundering down from the steep rock above her head.

It fell noisily into a churning pool below. The pool looked dangerous.

Ben and Zoe moved slowly around the narrow bank, the water swirling violently in the pool below their feet. Halfway around it, they stepped over a narrow stream that trickled downhill, away from the pool.

"Where does the rest of the water go?" Zoe asked. "There's a lot of water coming over the fall, but hardly any of it is going into the stream."

"Most of it must be draining into an underground river," Ben suggested. He peered into the undergrowth, looking for signs of black and white fur. As he parted a clump of bamboo stems, something the size of a large dog darted out of the thicket in a panic.

"It's only a musk deer," Zoe called to her brother.

"Did you see those long tusks?!" Ben said. "It was a male. The females —"

"Save the lecture until later," Zoe told him. "We need to stay focused on the panda hunt."

Zoe grabbed Ben's arm. "There's something moving over there," she said, pointing into the darkness. "See? By the fallen tree trunk."

Something was shuffling slowly among the small, craggy rocks that were scattered in the undergrowth. Through their goggles, they could just make out the occasional glimpse of light markings.

The shape stopped and plopped to the ground.

"It's a panda!" whispered Ben. "I caught a glimpse of a black eye patch."

"It must be Jing-Jing!" exclaimed Zoe.

Ben put his goggles on zoom. "I can't quite see it," he said. "It's half hidden behind the rocks."

They moved closer, stopping a short distance away from the panda. They squatted down between two big boulders.

Ben peered over the rock in front of them. When he crouched back down again, his face looked solemn. He didn't want to have to tell his sister what he'd just seen.

CHAPTER 8

WILD PANDA CHASE

"What's wrong?" Zoe asked Ben. "Is he hurt?"

"That's not Jing-Jing," said Ben slowly. "It's a wild panda."

Zoe stood and looked. At the foot of a tree trunk sat a huge adult panda. It was leaning against the tree, happily cleaning its belly. It was oblivious to Ben and Zoe.

Zoe felt sick with despair. She'd been so sure they'd found the lost cub.

"There's one good thing about this," said Ben, trying to cheer her up. "That panda looked healthy. It must have found another patch of bamboo nearby. That means Jing-Jing's probably eating healthy here."

Zoe smiled weakly. "I hope you're —" she began.

A ghostly cry filled the air. "It's the leopard again," warned Ben. "And it's really close. Look at the panda."

The panda stopped cleaning and scampered away into the undergrowth.

"The leopard won't be after us," said Zoe. "We have no scent. But it might be tracking Jing-Jing. He's young and weak — he'll be easy prey."

Zoe jumped up to scramble over the rock. "Come on, we've got to keep searching," she said. "We've wasted so much time already."

Zoe's foot missed her mark, and she slipped, banging her knee hard against the rock. She slumped to the ground with a yelp.

Ben ran to her. "Are you okay?" he asked.

"I'm fine," said Zoe, rubbing her leg. "We're not stopping now."

"Yes, we are," Ben said firmly. "It's too dangerous to go any farther tonight. If that leopard out there in the dark sees us, we'll be his dinner."

"But we can't just leave Jing-Jing out there," Zoe said, her voice quivering.

"What good would it do him if we fell down a ravine or ended up in the belly of a big cat?" Ben asked. He put his hand on Zoe's shoulder. "Look, there's a ledge of rock hanging over those pine trees. We can get some sleep underneath it and resume our search again in the morning. The scent dispersers should prevent the leopard from finding us."

Zoe nodded. Ben got out the sleeping bags and laid them on the forest floor beneath the open cave. "It's not going to get that cold overnight," Zoe said.

"But we'll want some sort of protection from water, and Erika said these are waterproof," Ben said. He kicked aside piles of sharp pine needles. "Don't want these as a mattress, though," he joked. Zoe didn't laugh.

There were two of Mr. Zhi's pancake wraps left. Ben passed one to Zoe. "Eat," he said. But Zoe only picked at it.

"There's no way I'll be able to sleep," she told Ben, handing him the leftover food. "I'm too worried about Jing-Jing." She climbed into her sleeping bag and stretched out, using her backpack as a pillow.

"Do you want a drink?" asked Ben, holding out his water bottle.

There was no reply. Zoe was already asleep. Ben let out a sigh of relief and smiled.

CHAPTER 9

CALLS OF THE WILD

Zoe suddenly awoke to find two eyes staring back at her. She tried to move but something was pressing on her chest. *Oh no,* she thought. *Was it the clouded leopard?* She could feel her heart thudding as the strange shape came slowly into focus in the pale morning light.

A golden snub-nosed monkey was looking down at her, its head tilted to one side. Zoe burst out laughing, sending the monkey scrambling for cover.

"What's going on?" Ben groaned, opening his eyes. "I was having a great dream. We were eating a nice, warm breakfast."

"This is the best I can do," Zoe said, holding up a squashed Nutrobar. "Field rations. Not the tastiest, but they'll keep our stomachs from growling — and frightening away all the wildlife."

They sat and munched on the fruit bars and gulped water to wash them down.

Birds overhead called to each other with whistles and screeches.

"I'll probably be hungry again in five minutes," said Ben. "Don't be surprised if I start gnawing on a tree or something."

Zoe rolled her eyes. "Do you ever stop thinking about food?" she asked.

Ben smirked. "Yeah," he said, "when I'm eating."

Zoe chuckled. She rolled up her sleeping bag, then checked her watch. "It's six in the morning," she said. "Let's get searching!" She peered out into the early morning mist. "If only we had an automatic panda finder."

Ben grinned. "Hold on," he said, pretending to search through his backpack, "I'm sure Uncle Stephen packed one of those for us."

Zoe shoved him playfully. Ben shoved her back. Zoe rolled away, giggling. Then she came to a stop. She scrambled to her knees and stared closely at the ground.

"I found another print!" she said.

"Not falling for one of your tricks," said Ben. "You're just going to trip me or something."

"I wouldn't joke about this," insisted Zoe. "Look!"

Keeping one eye on his sister and ready for any ambush, Ben crouched to inspect the ground. "A rear footprint with only three claws," he said. "We're on Jing-Jing's trail again!"

"Got another one," called Zoe from under a bush. "And another! They're fresh — and aiming toward the waterfall."

"There are tracks over here, too," said Ben. "But they're not panda prints. They have four toes and a roundish pad."

He aimed his BUG at them. It beeped after a few moments. "Clouded leopard!" Ben said, reading the display. "And it seems to be heading in the same direction as Jing-Jing."

BUG SAT MAP

FOREST

PINE TREES

ROCK

DEAD BAMBOO

Zoe joined him. "It looks like Jing-Jing is being stalked," she said grimly. "Let's hope we can pinpoint his location before the leopard finds him."

"I know a good search pattern for us to follow," said Ben, checking his BUG's map.

WATERFALL

POOL

DENSE
FOREST

N

STREAM

"We'll check out the area around the pool in a semicircle, moving toward it as we go," Ben suggested. "That way, we'll have the best chance of finding him."

Using the BUG map to plot their course, Ben and Zoe advanced, side by side, through the forest. They pushed aside ferns and bushes and peered into all the shadowy places where a panda could hide.

Zoe came to a sudden halt and listened intently. "What's that noise?" she asked.

Ben stopped next to her. "Sounds like a small dog barking," he said.

Zoe clutched Ben's arm. "They're from a panda!" she realized.

Ben quickly pressed a key on his BUG to identify the animal call.

"We'll have to get closer," Ben said, holding his BUG up high. "The BUG's not picking up the sound from here."

"It's coming from that direction," said Zoe, pointing to the densest part of the forest.

Zoe plunged into the dark undergrowth, pausing every now and again to check the direction of the sound. She turned to find Ben waving his BUG at her. "You were right," he said. "I'm picking it up now. It is a panda!"

After he spoke, the call faded and stopped. "Did we scare him away?" whispered Zoe.

Ben frowned. "Or he was attacked," he said. "Then again, I haven't heard the leopard since last night."

They crept among the ferns and branches, trying not to crunch on the cones and twigs underfoot. They moved closer to where the call had come from. Red-backed beetles and small spiders scuttled out from underneath their feet as they walked.

"Why can't we find him?" said Zoe. "He has to be nearby."

"You know what Grandma says when we can't find something," said Ben. "You haven't looked in the right place."

"But we have," said Zoe. "Jing-Jing's either gone or he's really well hidden somewhere in here." She dug into her backpack and slipped on the thermogoggles that Erika had given them. "I wonder if we're close enough to use these."

Ben pulled his on and slowly scanned the area. "Wow!" he exclaimed.

Through the glasses, he could see the shapes of creatures moving through the forest. Their bodies glowed purple, yellow and orange. "I didn't realize there was so much animal life around!" Ben said.

"Concentrate, Ben!" Zoe said. "Do you see anything that looks like a panda?"

Ben shook his head. "Nothing yet," he said. "Monkeys of all sizes, parrots . . ."

"There's something big right over there," said Zoe, pointing. They both took off their glasses. "Behind that dead tree stump."

Watching and listening for any sounds, Ben and Zoe moved cautiously toward the tall, wide tree. When they reached it, they slowly peered around it. "Nothing there," Zoe said, sighing.

"Were the goggles wrong?" asked Ben.

Ben pulled his thermogoggles over his eyes and checked again. Then he stopped and stared hard at the tree trunk.

"There is something here," he whispered. "Something big. And it's inside the tree!"

Ben tried to find his flashlight, but Zoe quickly pulled him back away from the stump. "We have to be careful," she said. "It could be anything — we've heard leopard calls, remember?"

There was a sudden movement from the dead tree. Ben and Zoe ripped off their goggles and took cover behind some plants. "It has round black ears," whispered Ben. "That's no leopard."

The top of a furry head appeared. "And a white face," Zoe whispered back. "It's definitely a panda. It has to be Jing-Jing this time!"

"Don't get your hopes up," murmured Ben as two black eye patches slowly appeared.

"It looks like a cub," said Zoe. She watched the slow-moving animal closely. "If it is Jing-Jing, I bet he was hiding from the leopard."

The panda climbed clumsily out of its hole, grunting painfully as it moved. It plopped to the ground and rested against the tree. Slowly turning its head, it scanned the dense forest. Its ears twitched as if it were listening closely for something.

"Let's get a little closer," Ben whispered in Zoe's ear. "If it's Jing-Jing, he won't be scared. He's used to being around people."

With their hearts beating loudly in their ears, they moved closer to the young panda. At first the cub didn't move.

It gazed from Zoe to Ben, panting heavily. "It looks undernourished," whispered Ben. "Its belly isn't round, and its eyes look dull."

Zoe kneeled down in front of the little panda. "Don't be scared," she said. "We won't hurt you." She looked up at Ben. "I can't see its back paws. We still don't know if it's Jing-Jing."

Ben slid a hand into his backpack. "Jing-Jing or not, it needs our help," he said.

Ben broke off a piece of panda bread and handed it to Zoe. The panda flinched at the movement, then scrambled to its feet. Within seconds, it had disappeared into the trees.

"That must have been a wild panda," said Ben. "Jing-Jing wouldn't have been frightened like that."

"It was Jing-Jing," said Zoe, jumping up. "I saw his paw as he went. It only had three toes."

"Then why did he run away from us?" asked Ben.

"I think it might be the scent dispersers," Zoe reminded him. "We might have looked like humans, but we didn't smell familiar to him. He was probably confused. Anyway, follow me. The tracks are heading back to the area with the dead bamboo."

They followed the line of tracks downhill through the brown, withered stalks. At first, the tracks led in a straight line, but then the steps seemed to weave back and forth unsteadily.

"I bet it was just the adrenaline burst from being afraid that gave him the energy to run away," said Ben as he examined the prints. "He'll be more exhausted than ever now — and easy prey for the leopard."

"We have to find him first," said Zoe as they tiptoed forward. "But this time we take it really slowly. No sudden movements — and turn our scent dispersers off."

They could hear the waterfall crashing in the distance somewhere above them. The trees thinned a little, and the prints led to a narrow stream.

Something was moving on the other side of the the ferns. It was taking slow, labored steps. It barely had enough energy to keep moving. Suddenly, it stopped and slumped to the ground.

"Now's our chance," said Ben. "Remember, no sudden movements."

"Come on," said Zoe, peering out. "We need to help him."

"No," said Ben. Zoe could hear tension in his voice. "Look up there."

Zoe followed his gaze. Crouched on a branch above Jing-Jing was a snarling leopard. Its coat, dark and blotched like a snake, rippled as its muscles tightened.

Zoe gasped. "It's going to pounce on Jing-Jing!" she whispered.

But the leopard's head suddenly whipped around, its ears twitching wildly. "What's the matter with it?" whispered Ben. Then the forest came alive with anxious bird calls and monkey cries. The leopard let out a strange, high-pitched yowl. Then it streaked off and disappeared.

RUMBLE! A deafening sound rose up from under them. It sounded as if rocks were being smashed together. With a tremendous flutter of wings, the birds left the trees. Distant cries of terrified animals filled the forest. Zoe was thrown off her feet.

Zoe crashed into Ben, and they both went sprawling. "Take cover!" Ben shouted.

Zoe made herself into a tight ball and covered her head. Ben dived down next to her, holding his backpack above them.

Stones and small boulders tumbled down the hill and bounced over them. Ben could feel the rocks striking his backpack. Luckily, it cushioned the heavy blows.

Then, as suddenly as it had started, the aftershock stopped. "Thanks, Ben," Zoe said gratefully. "That was some quick thinking."

"And that was some aftershock!" said Ben.

Zoe scrambled to her feet. "Where's Jing-Jing?" she said, scanning the forest. "I don't see him."

Ben pointed to some bushes. "He's taken shelter over there," he said. The little panda lay under the overhanging leaves, his head slumped down on his chest.

"We have to get to him," said Zoe, urgently tugging at Ben's arm.

"Agreed," said Ben. "But we don't know if the leopard's still around."

They were about to jump across the narrow stream when more rumbling filled the air. "What's that?" cried Zoe, stopping suddenly. "Is it another aftershock?"

"The ground's not shaking this time," Ben said. He peered up the slope of the mountain.

"It's coming from the direction of the waterfall," Ben said. "It's as if the entire mountainside itself is roaring."

A noise like an explosion hit their ears as water burst out from the slope above. The rushing water flattened trees and bushes in its wake as it surged down the hillside in a deafening torrent. It brought dirt, rocks, and branches along with it. Ben and Zoe stumbled back in terror as the wall of water pounded into the narrow stream. Entire trees were slipping down the slope toward them. Ben pulled Zoe farther back from the shifting earth.

"The aftershock caused this!" Ben said as a huge boulder went crashing past them.

Horrified, Ben and Zoe gazed down the steep, sloping bank at their feet.

Below them, the raging river swept away rocks and wood as it rushed wildly downhill. Jing-Jing was motionless under the branches on the opposite side. The ground was much lower there, and he was within a few feet of the deadly flow.

"If the earth crumbles any more than it has, he'll be swept away," Zoe said. "And there's no way we can get across to him!"

"I have an idea," said Ben, looking determined. "We need to make a bridge!"

"There are uprooted trees everywhere," said Zoe, nodding. "But they'd all be too heavy for us to move."

Ben gritted his teeth. "Then we'll swing across," he said.

"We can't," said Zoe. She thought for a moment. "But we can zip wire! Our bank's higher than Jing-Jing's, and Uncle Stephen gave us those Fisher Integrated Nanofirers, remember?" She pulled her FIN out of her backpack. "Erika told me about it on the plane. There's a nanocord inside."

"Sounds great," Ben said, "but how are we going to see a cord that thin?"

"It glows," said Zoe impatiently. "And before you ask me, I don't have time to explain it to you."

Zoe glanced across the river. "We just need something on both sides of the river to attach the cord to," she said. "That tree trunk over there just beyond Jing-Jing looks strong enough to support us."

"But how will we get it over there?" Ben asked.

"Erika said there's a dart on the end of the cord," Zoe said. "The FIN will shoot it into the wood and make sure it holds tight."

She aimed the end of the flashlight-like gadget over the river and pressed a button on the tube.

An object shot out of the FIN and sped across the raging river, carrying a red glowing wire with it.

The dart embedded itself in the trunk. Zoe turned around and slammed the other end of the FIN against the tree behind her. There was a thud as something inside it rammed into the bark. "That locked it into position," she said. "Now we can use it as a zip line."

"Sweet!" said Ben. "This hook on the top of my backpack must be used to attach to the line."

Zoe saw the gleam in Ben's eye that meant he was about to do something reckless. Ben tightened his backpack and grasped the metal hook and clipped himself to the wire. "See you on the other side!" he said, sailing into the air.

"Wait," cried Zoe in alarm. "We haven't tested it yet!"

"No time!" Ben said. He sped down the wire.

CHAPTER 10
TRAPPED?

Ben plunged down the mountainside. His eyes went wide as the tree sped towards him. "Uh oh," he said. *THUMP!* He smashed into the tree, the jolt traveling through his body.

"Ow," Ben said, rubbing his forehead. He reached up, unclipped his backpack from the wire, and dropped to the ground. He immediately ran to the panda. Jing-Jing wasn't moving. He didn't even seem to be breathing.

Ben saw Zoe flash past. He turned to watch as she gracefully dismounted before hitting the tree.

Zoe tucked, rolled onto her back, and sprang to her feet in one graceful movement.

Ben couldn't hide his awe. "Nice moves, sis," he said.

"Thanks," Zoe said. "Now maybe next time you'll listen to me before you get impulsive." She removed her harness and kneeled next to Ben.

Zoe stroked the panda's head gently. "Jing-Jing," she whispered. "We've come to take you home." Zoe glanced up at Ben, tears welling in her eyes. "Are we too late?"

Suddenly, Jing-Jing let out a ragged breath. "He's alive!" Zoe cried. "Quick, pass me his feeding bottle."

Ben tossed the bottle to Zoe. She put the mouthpiece to Jing-Jing's lips. At first, nothing happened. But as Jing-Jing's eyes slowly opened, his mouth began to close feebly around the bottle.

"Go on, Jing-Jing," urged Zoe. "Drink."

The panda took a spluttering mouthful, followed by another.

Then, with faint grunts, he began to gulp down the fluid. Zoe gently eased the bottle from his mouth. "Slowly now," she said gently. "Your body's not used to it."

Suddenly, the ground beneath their feet began to crumble away as the force of the water battered against the earth. Ben and Zoe leaped up and took Jing-Jing by the front legs. They pulled with all their strength, barely managing to drag him to safety before the water swept violently past.

The ground where they'd been sitting was swept downriver.

"That was close!" said Ben. "Jing-Jing may be starving, but he still weighs a lot. We'll never be able to carry him down the mountain. We have to call Uncle Stephen right away." He pressed the key on his BUG that called WILD Headquarters.

Jing-Jing lay on the ground, trembling. Zoe helped him to sit up, tucking her sleeping bag behind him to support his back. She pulled out some panda bread, soaked it in the water, and touched it to his lips. But the panda cub didn't seem to notice.

"Ben, good to hear from you!" Uncle Stephen's voice burst out. "What do you have to report?"

"We've located Jing-Jing!" Ben called into the speaker.

"Good work!" Uncle Stephen said, sounding delighted.

"He's very weak," Ben said into his BUG. "And we can't transport him back to Ningshang by ourselves."

"Not surprised," came their uncle's voice. "He likely weighs as much as you do!"

Ben frowned. "Twice as much," he said.

"Don't worry," their uncle said. "I will let the sanctuary know where to find him — anonymously, of course. Just make sure they don't see you when they arrive! Over and out."

Ben kneeled next to Jing-Jing. "Now all we can do is keep our little friend safe," he said, "and wait."

"Remember how long it took us to get up here?" said Zoe. "The rescuers are going to take forever to arrive." She offered the panda another drink, but his head flopped back down to his chest weakly.

"But they know exactly where to come," Ben reminded her.

Zoe suddenly stiffened. "We've got company," she said, pointing across the river.

The clouded leopard was prowling
up and down the other side of the bank,
watching them. Ben and Zoe sat perfectly
still.

"It can't reach us," whispered Zoe, "but
it's still scary."

"Do you think it's been hunting Jing-Jing
this whole time?" asked Ben.

"I don't know," said Zoe, stroking the
panda's head. "I'm just glad we got to him
first."

Ben smirked. "I'm just glad we've got a raging river between us and that leopard," he said.

Just then, the leopard stopped pacing. It cautiously made its way down toward the water.

"Leopards don't swim," Zoe said uncertainly. She looked at Ben, hoping for confirmation. "Right?"

The leopard seemed to consider swimming, but then backed away from the rushing river. It stared at them hungrily for a moment, then slowly crept away until it was just a shadow against the undergrowth. After a moment, it left.

Ben and Zoe sat on both sides of Jing-Jing, trying to keep him warm until the sanctuary arrived. The little panda's breathing was shallow.

Ben's BUG gave out a chirp. He jumped to his feet and waved it at his sister. "Look at this," he said, alarmed. "The satellite map has updated. This water made a wide barrier right down into the valley and over to the river. The rescuers might get here in time, but they'll be stuck on the other side!"

Zoe's eyes went wide. "Then there's no way the rescuers can get to Jing-Jing," she said.

Ben nodded. Zoe tucked the warm sleeping bag around Jing-Jing. "Don't worry, Jing-Jing," she said. "We'll think of something."

"We have to get back to the other side somehow," muttered Ben.

"No way!" said his sister. "The leopard could return at any time!"

"We'll have to risk it," Ben said.

"Even if we could get across, we'd never be able to take Jing-Jing with us," Zoe said. "We've got to stay here, Ben."

Ben was deep in thought. "Too bad we can't just use the zip line to go uphill," he said. "Wait — I've still got my FIN!"

Zoe narrowed her eyes. "Yes, but I don't see how —" she began.

"The RETRACT button!" Ben said excitedly.

He dumped everything out of his backpack until he found his FIN. He aimed it across the river and up at the tree where Zoe's FIN was already bolted. The dart zipped over the water, and settled deep in the trunk. He tested the glowing cord with a tug.

"You haven't thought this through," Zoe said. "We have two uphill cords to get us — and a heavy panda — across to the other side. It can't be done."

"Yes it can," said Ben. "We need to make a sling for Jing-Jing with the rope and a sleeping bag and attach it to your nanocord. We both climb on with him, and then I tie this end of my FIN on to the sling and press retract. That should pull us across."

Ben stood tall and pointed out his Fin. "Watch!" he said, pressing the RETRACT button. Immediately, the cord retracted and he was jerked forward onto his stomach and dragged toward the river. Zoe shouted in alarm. Ben frantically pressed the switch again, and he came to a halt at the edge of the fiercely flowing river.

"Well, I've proved it's powerful," Ben said shakily. He stood up and backed away from the bank. Then he bent down and gave Jing-Jing a gentle pat. "You're going for a little ride, my friend."

"I hope this works," muttered Zoe. She grabbed Ben's sleeping bag and laid it on the ground underneath the zip line. With a lot of effort, they managed to roll Jing-Jing's heavy body onto the bag. He barely moved.

Ben took two ropes from his backpack and threaded one through the eyelets in the top corners of the sleeping bag. He weaved the second rope through the eyelets at the bottom. "Now we have to tie the ropes to the nanocord," he said. "You take the top and I'll take the bottom. That will lift Jing-Jing off the ground."

Zoe nodded. Then Ben said, "Ready? Pull!"

Jing-Jing was suspended above the ground in his makeshift sling. Ben climbed on at the front, next to the panda cub's head. He tied the strap of his FIN firmly to one of the sling ropes.

"You ride by his feet," Ben told his sister. Zoe climbed on behind and held on tight. The sling rocked with her weight, but the ropes held firm.

"Are you sure about this, Ben?" asked Zoe. "We might all end up falling in the river."

"It's Jing-Jing's only chance," insisted Ben. "Hang on tight — and here we go!"

Ben pressed the retract button. They were jerked forward as the nanocord wound itself back inside the gadget. "It's working!" Ben shouted.

With the FIN whirring madly, they found themselves being pulled out over the tumbling water as the nanocord retracted. Zoe glanced down at the raging river below them. It made her feel sick to think of them plummeting down into the water below.

Zoe gripped the sling ropes tightly and kept her eyes focused on the bank opposite.

"We're almost there!" Ben shouted to his sister.

Then they felt a sudden jolt. "What's happened?" cried Zoe. "We stopped!"

Ben pressed the RETRACT button again and again. "It's broken," he called. "We're stuck."

"Can you jump to the bank from here?" Zoe asked. "Then pull us in the rest of the way?"

"I'll try," Ben said. He eased himself over the ledge of the bank.

"Be careful!" Zoe called out.

Ben released his grip and pushed. He half-jumped, half-fell toward the high bank.

As he soared over the water, he knew he wasn't going to make it. His legs plunged into the water, and the cold current sucked at him as he desperately clutched a tangled root. He kicked his feet up and managed to get his knees into a hole in the bank. Slowly and carefully, he hauled himself up onto the ground and collapsed, exhausted.

"Ben!" Zoe yelled. Her voice sounded strange. Ben looked up.

The clouded leopard was back. It was crouched on the bank, less than ten feet away from him. Its belly was on the ground as it slinked slowly and deliberately toward him. Ben's heart was beating so fast that he thought it would burst out of his chest. Any moment now, the leopard was going to leap — and there was nothing he could do about it. Desperate, Ben grabbed a stone and threw it at the beast.

The leopard flinched back as the stone struck the ground in front of it. Then it tensed, ready to attack.

Suddenly, the air was filled with a tremendous roar. The leopard whipped around, its ears twitching wildly.

Horrified, Ben followed its gaze. "It can't be," he whispered.

A huge tiger was standing on the bank a few feet away, with its teeth bared. The leopard gave a yowl of terror and sprinted away. The tiger turned its head toward Ben. Its fierce, golden eyes glared down at him. *I'm dead meat,* Ben thought.

But then, to Ben's utter astonishment, the tiger turned away and disappeared into the shadows. Completely confused, Ben looked up at Zoe. Then he understood what had happened.

Zoe was holding her BUG and directing it toward where the tiger had been.

"It was a holo-image!" Ben said. "Brilliant idea, Zoe! You saved my life."

"No problem," Zoe said, smiling. "But if you want to pay me back, perhaps you'd like to pull us to the bank somehow?"

Ben looked around the bank. He picked up a sturdy branch. "Hold onto this," he called. Zoe reached for the stick, and managed to grip it tightly.

Ben pulled with all his strength. Slowly, the sling began to move forward. A moment later it was hovering over the bank, just a few inches from the ground. Zoe jumped down and helped Ben untie the ropes. They lowered the sling to the ground. Jing-Jing rolled out with a faint groan.

"We made it!" exclaimed Zoe. "I just hope Jing-Jing's all right."

As she kneeled next to the panda cub to check on him, there was a sudden shout from the forest. Ben and Zoe looked at each other. "We've got to hide!" Ben said.

"And make sure we leave nothing behind," added Zoe. She twisted her FIN to eject it from the tree. Then she held the two buttons down and the dart on the other side of the river was released. Her cord flew back into her gizmo, now fully retracted. But Ben's FIN was still dead.

"There's no way we can cut this nanocord," he said. "I'm going to have to ditch my FIN." He slung the gizmo high up into the tree, leaving no sign of it.

They snatched up their backpacks along with the sleeping bag.

Ben and Zoe dived into the bushes just as a woman in a blue sanctuary sweatshirt burst onto the bank. She shouted something in Sichuanese.

"Put your translator in!" Zoe whispered.

"Jing-Jing's here!" they heard the woman shout. Three men and another woman ran up and kneeled next to Jing-Jing, dropping their bags next to them.

"He's still alive!" one person said. Someone else opened a medical box.

"Only barely," another sanctuary member said. "His pulse is very weak."

"I wonder who sent that message," one of the workers said. "I don't see anybody around here." Ben and Zoe shrank back into the shadows as the worker scanned the trees.

"Well," a man said, "the important thing is we got to Jing-Jing in time."

They gently eased the little panda on to a stretcher. They attached an IV drip with a bag of clear fluid to his leg. A woman stood beside the stretcher, holding the bag up.

Moments later, the rescue party disappeared, carrying the panda cub back home. Ben and Zoe emerged from their hiding place. "Jing-Jing's in good hands now," said Zoe. "I think he's going to be okay."

CHAPTER 11

SANCTUARY

Ben and Zoe emerged from the shadowy forest and into the sunshine. They were near the site of the new medical center. Just beyond, they could see the roof of their hotel. Behind them, the water from the landslide plunged down the hill on its way to merge with the river.

Ben's BUG vibrated. "It's Uncle Stephen!" he said, glancing at the display.

"Hey, kids!" their uncle said. His voice came out loud and clear. "Any news?"

"The sanctuary members made it up the mountain," Zoe reported. "Now we're on our way to check on Jing-Jing."

"Yes," said Uncle Stephen. "I made sure they got to him."

"But what did you tell them?" asked Ben. "I mean, who did you say you were?"

"I said, 'Hello there, I'm Dr. Fisher, head of a top-secret organization . . .'" Uncle Stephen said. Zoe and Ben's eyes went wide. Then they heard their uncle chuckling. "I'm just kidding. Don't you worry, I just said I was with the government and that the sanctuary had better not ask any questions."

Ben and Zoe were silent. Their uncle was a little weird sometimes. "Anyway, good job!" their uncle said. "See you upon your return!" The call ended.

"He sure has a strange way of doing things," said Zoe with a grin.

Ben pocketed his BUG. "Yeah," he agreed, "but they always seem to work!"

"Yeah," Zoe agreed. "He always comes through."

"I can't believe how tired I am," groaned Zoe. "My legs have never ached so much."

"What do you expect?" Ben said, laughing. "We've walked for miles, narrowly missed a landslide, gotten stuck on a zip line, escaped from a leopard, and rescued a chubby panda. Of course you're tired!" He looked slyly at his sister. "But are you too tired to go to the sanctuary and find out how Jing-Jing's doing?"

Zoe's eyes sparkled. "Of course not!" she exclaimed. "In fact, I'll race you there!"

Laughing together, they sprinted down the slope.

Soon, they were at the gate of the sanctuary. "I just had a scary thought," said Zoe, pulling at Ben's sleeve. "Do you think Xu Mei will want to see us?"

"She did seem pretty upset yesterday," Ben agreed. "Let's just go and ask about Jing-Jing and see what happens."

A man was coming toward them carrying buckets of vegetables. "Excuse me," called Zoe. "We were wondering if the little panda has been found."

The man looked them up and down, a shocked expression on his face. Ben and Zoe suddenly realized how dirty and dishevelled they were. Zoe pulled a twig out of Ben's hair.

"We fell down a hole," Ben said nervously.

The man put down his buckets and scratched his head. "I don't understand," he said at last. "My English is not good."

"Jing-Jing?" Zoe prompted him.

"Ah, yes!" the man said. "He is —"

A happy cry came from the infirmary. "Zoe! Ben!" It was Xu Mei, smiling from ear to ear. "Jing-Jing's back, and he's going to be all right!"

Xu Mei grabbed their hands and took them inside the building. She led them to a room at the end. She knocked on the door and stuck her head inside. Then the door opened wide, and Xu Mei's father stood before them."Come in," he said warmly. "Meet our naughty runaway panda cub!"

A woman was leaning over a large plastic cot. There, lying on a blanket and with the IV tube still in his leg, lay Jing-Jing.

At once, Zoe and Ben could see there was more life in his eyes.

He was sucking noisily at a bottle of milk. As soon as he caught sight of them he gave an excited little squeak.

"He likes you two!" said Xu Mei.

"He looks a lot better than . . ." began Zoe. Ben coughed loudly. ". . . Better than I expected him to!" Zoe finished nervously.

"He's getting water and food in the drip," said Xu Mei. "Father doesn't want him eating too quickly. His stomach has shrunk and it will make him sick. But he loves milk, so we couldn't say no."

They stood at the panda's side, stroking his ears while he greedily gulped down his milk. Soon, his eyes grew heavy, the bottle fell to his side, and he began to snore.

"Look, Ben," Zoe teased. "He falls asleep after pigging out — just like you!"

Ben rolled his eyes. "Really funny, Zoe," he said.

Xu Mei chuckled. "We should let him sleep now," she said.

Out in the corridor, Zoe took Xu Mei's hand. "I hope you've forgiven us for not going into the mountains with you yesterday."

The little girl looked at her gravely. "I was being silly," she said. "You were right, it was too dangerous for me to go up there."

"That's very true," said Ben, giving his sister a knowing glance. Zoe winked back at Ben.

"If only I knew who found Jing-Jing," Xu Mei went on. "I really want to say thank you."

"I'm sure his rescuers know how grateful you are," said Zoe.

Suddenly, Xu Mei turned and stared intently at Ben and Zoe's filthy clothing.

"I was just thinking," Xu Mei said, her eyes wide. "Jing-Jing did his happy cry when he saw you. It was like he had met you before."

"But that's impossible," said Ben.

Xu Mei nodded. "Yes," she said. A huge smile spread over her face. "Impossible."

They peered through the glass door of the infirmary. Jing-Jing lay peacefully asleep in his cot. Xu Mei sighed happily.

"There's one thing his rescuers can be sure of," said Zoe. "Jing-Jing is the most loved panda in the whole wide world."

THE AUTHORS

Jan Burchett and **Sara Vogler** were already
friends when they discovered they both wanted
to write children's books, and that it was much
more fun to do it together. They have since written
over a hundred and thirty stories ranging from
educational books and stories for younger readers
to young adult fiction. They have written for series
such as Dinosaur Cove and Beast Quest, and they
are authors of the Gargoylz books.

THE ILLUSTRATOR

Diane Le Feyer discovered a passion for drawing
and animation at the age of five. In 2002, she
graduated with honors from the Ecole Emile Cohl
school of design. Diane worked as a character
designer, 3D modeler, and animator in the video
games industry before joining the Cartoon Saloon
animation studio, where she worked as a director,
animator, illustrator, and character designer. Diane
was also a part of the early design and development
of the movie *The Secret of Kells*.

GLOSSARY

adrenaline (uh-DREN-uh-lin)—a chemical produced by your body when you are excited, angry, or frightened

aftershock (AF-turh-shok)—an earthquake that comes soon after a stronger earthquake in the same general location

ascent (uh-SENT)—moving upward

briefing (BREEF-ing)—a meeting where someone is given information so they can carry out a task or mission

compound (KOM-pound)—an area of land that is usually fenced in

endangered (en-DAYN-jurd)—at risk of going extinct

intel (IN-tel)—information

mission (MISH-uhn)—a special job or task

operative (OP-ur-uh-tiv)—a secret agent

sanctuary (SANGK-choo-er-ee)—a natural area where animals are protected from hunters

shattered (SHAT-urd)—broke into tiny pieces

vibrated (VYE-brate-id)—moved back and forth rapidly

THE GIANT PANDA
STATUS: ENDANGERED

Giant pandas were once widespread in China, but now they are only found in the southwest. Several threats have contributed to their dwindling numbers:

DEFORESTATION: Giant pandas live in mountainous areas that have bamboo forests. These areas are threatened by logging and road building. Destruction of pandas' habitat is the biggest threat to their survival.

STARVATION: Bamboo plants take a long time to grow. Pandas need to eat many pounds of bamboo each day in order to sustain themselves. Because of deforestation, there are fewer bamboo plants in the wild than there used to be.

LOW REPRODUCTION: Pandas live for about 20 years in the wild, and 30 years in captivity. However, they have not adapted to living in captivity and do not mate often enough to quickly increase their numbers. When they do have cubs, pandas typically only have one or two babies per litter.

PREDATORS: Jackals and leopards prey on giant pandas.

POACHERS: Panda fur is very soft and is coveted by poachers.

BUT THERE'S STILL HOPE FOR THE GIANT PANDA! The Chinese government has established many reserves located in the pandas' natural habitat, and bamboo is being replanted all over the reserves. Scientists are also learning more and more about panda mating habits, and poaching has declined due to new, harsher penalties.

DISCUSSION QUESTIONS

1. The giant panda is one of Zoe's favorite animals. What's your favorite animal? Why?

2. Do you think Ben and Zoe are heroes? Why or why not?

3. There are many illustrations in this book. Which one is your favorite? Why?

WRITING PROMPTS

1. Ben and Zoe are operatives for a secret environmental organization called WILD. Think up your own secret organization. What is your organization's name? What causes does your organization support? How will you further your cause? Write about it.

2. Ben and Zoe are trusted by their Uncle Stephen. Who do you trust? Who trusts you? What makes a person trustworthy? Write about trust.

3. Zoe and Ben use several high-tech gadgets in this story. Invent your own gadget. What does it do? How will you use it? Write about your invention. Then draw a picture of it.